DRAGON'S
Halloween

DAV PILKEY

ᵁ ACORN™
SCHOLASTIC

For Herb Sandberg

Published in the UK by Scholastic Children's Books, 2020
Euston House, 24 Eversholt Street, London, NW1 1DB
A division of Scholastic Limited

London – New York – Toronto – Sydney – Auckland
Mexico City – New Delhi – Hong Kong

SCHOLASTIC and associated logos are trademarks and/or
registered trademarks of Scholastic Inc.

First published in the US by Orchard Books, 1993
This edition first published in the US by Scholastic Inc., 2020

Text and illustrations © Dav Pilkey, 1993, 2020
Book design by Dav Pilkey and Sarah Dvojack

The right of Dav Pilkey to be identified as the author and illustrator of this work
has been asserted by him under the Copyright, Designs and Patents Act 1988.

ISBN 978 0702 30194 0

A CIP catalogue record for this book is available from the British Library.

Printed by CPI Group (UK) Ltd, Croydon, CR0 4YY
Papers used by Scholastic Children's Books are made
from wood grown in sustainable forests.

1 3 5 7 9 10 8 6 4 2

www.scholastic.co.uk

Contents

1
Six Small Pumpkins

It was October,
and all the world was orange and brown.
Dragon walked through the autumn leaves
in search of a giant pumpkin.

2

"I will find a pumpkin as big as a house," said Dragon.
"Oh, what a scary jack-o'-lantern it will make."

3

But when Dragon got to the pumpkin patch,
all of the big pumpkins were already gone.
Only six small pumpkins were left,
and they were much too small to be scary.

Dragon loaded the six small
pumpkins into his cart
and brought them home anyway.

Later, as Dragon sat carving
his small pumpkins,
a fox and a crocodile came by.

"What are you doing?" asked the fox.

"I'm making scary jack-o'-lanterns,"
said Dragon.

"Those pumpkins are too small to be scary,"
said the fox.

"Just wait," said Dragon.

Dragon took one of the pumpkins
and poked branches into its sides.

"That pumpkin looks stupid,"
said the crocodile.
"No one will be afraid of your silly
jack-o'-lanterns!"

"Just wait," said Dragon.

Dragon put candles into the pumpkins,
and they all lit up bright and orange.

"Ha, ha, ha, ha, ha!" laughed the fox
and the crocodile.

"We've never seen such funny jack-o'-lanterns
in all our lives!"

"Just wait," said Dragon.

Finally, Dragon stacked the pumpkins
on top of one another
until they were very tall.

The fox and the crocodile
stopped laughing.
Their eyes became wide.
They began to tremble and shake.

"Ah...aaaaah!" cried the crocodile.

"Oh...oooooh!" wailed the fox.

13

The fox and the crocodile ran off
through the woods,
screaming in terror.

"What's the matter with them?"
said Dragon.

Dragon scratched his big head and looked up at the jack-o'-lanterns.

"Aaah! Eeeh! Aaah!" screamed Dragon.

Dragon ran into his house
and hid under the bed.

"I did not know
that six small pumpkins could be so scary!"
said Dragon.

2
The Costume Party

It was Halloween night,
and Dragon was very excited.
He had been invited to a
Halloween costume party.

Dragon tried to think of
a scary costume to wear.

Dragon could not decide whether to be
a witch, a vampire, or a mummy.
He thought and thought,
and scratched his big head.

"One costume would be very scary," said Dragon, "but **three** costumes would be very, **very**, VERY, scary!"

So Dragon decided to wear all three costumes at the same time.

VAMPIRE COSTUME

First, Dragon put on a witch's hat and nose.

"I feel scary already," said Dragon.

Next, Dragon put on a vampire's cape
and teeth.
Dragon could not talk very well
with vampire teeth in his mouth.
"Flmmm flmmm flbm mmm fmm,"
said Dragon.

Finally, Dragon wrapped himself up
just like a mummy.

Dragon hoped his costume would not be
too scary.

Dragon walked through the woods
to the big costume party.

Suddenly, the wind began to blow.

"FLASH!" went the lightning.

"BOOM!" went the thunder.

And DOWN came the rain.

29

When Dragon finally got to the party,
he was soaking wet,
and his costume was ruined.

All of the animals began to laugh.

"Look at Dragon!" they cried.
"Oh, what a silly costume!"

The animals laughed and laughed,
and Dragon felt terrible.
He walked over to a bench in the corner
and sat down next to a big pumpkin.

Suddenly, the bench broke, and the pumpkin flipped high into the air.

SPLAT!

Dragon was very dizzy.
He stumbled around the room
covered with slimy orange pumpkin goop.

When the animals saw Dragon,
they screamed in terror.

"**Eek! It's a monster!**" cried the duck,
who jumped into the pig's arms.

"Oh, dear! Oh, dear!" cried the pig,
who jumped into the hippo's arms.

"Help! Help! Help!" cried the hippo,
who jumped into the hamster's arms.

Finally, Dragon pulled the pumpkin
off his head.

"I am not a monster," said Dragon.
"I am only Dragon."

The animals were very relieved,
and soon everyone felt much better.

Well . . . **almost** everyone.

3
The Deep Dark Woods

The moon was full,
the sky was dark,
and the stomach was empty.

Dragon was **very** hungry.
He walked home through
the spooky forest
thinking of good things to eat.

Softly, the wind began to blow.
Whoo . . . whoooo . . .
WHoooowwWHHhooowHOOO.

That was a scary sound.

The wet leaves beneath Dragon's feet
went **squish, squish, squish, squish!**

That was a scarier sound.

When Dragon got farther into the forest, he heard the scariest sound of all.

"Grrr . . . grrr . . . GRROWWWL!"

For a moment, everything was silent. Then suddenly,

"Grrr . . . grrrr . . . GRRROWWWWL!"

"What could that awful noise be?" cried Dragon.

"Grrrrr . . . grrrrr . . . GRRRROWWWWWL!"

The growling got louder and louder.

"GRRRR . . . GRRRRRRRRR . . .
GRRRRRRROWWWWWWWWWWWL!"

Finally, Dragon jumped in the air.

"Help me!" he screamed.
"It's a **monster!**"

High up in the treetops,
a light flicked on.

"What's going on down there?"
shouted a sleepy-eyed squirrel.

"I hear a monster growling!"
cried Dragon.

"That's no monster," yelled the squirrel.
"That's your **stomach**!"

"Now go home and get something to eat
before you wake up the whole forest!"
cried the angry squirrel.

Dragon held his stomach.
It rumbled and growled.
He felt very silly.

All at once, the forest was dark again.
But now, Dragon was too hungry
to be afraid.
He ran and ran all the way home.

When Dragon got home,
he cooked up a giant Halloween feast.
He made pumpkin pies,
pumpkin soup,
pumpkin bread,
pumpkin pizzas,
and pumpkin ice-cream sundaes.

Then, Dragon ate and ate and ate . . .

. . .until he was as round as a pumpkin.

About the Author

DAV PILKEY is the writer and illustrator of the worldwide bestselling Dog Man and Captain Underpants series. He has written and illustrated many other books for young readers, including the Caldecott Honor book *The Paperboy*, *Dog Breath*, and *The Hallo-Wiener*. Dav lives in the Pacific Northwest with his wife.

YOU CAN DRAW DRAGON!

1 Draw a heart shape, but leave the bottom open.

2 Add Dragon's eyes, nose, and mouth. Put two horns on top of his head.

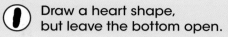

3 Draw Dragon's back, tail, and tummy. Then add his arm and leg.

4 Draw spikes down his back and on his tail. Don't forget to add his other arm and leg too!

5 Draw grass and a tower of circles.

6 Add buttons to the three bottom circles. Draw a face on the top three circles. Add two stems for horns.

7 Add arms to the jack-o'-lantern. It is so spooky!

8 Colour in your drawing!

WHAT'S YOUR STORY?

Dragon makes a scary costume for the party.
Imagine **you** are going to a costume party.
What costume would you wear?
How would you make it?
Write and draw your story!

BONUS!

Try making your story just like Dav —
with watercolours! Did you know that
Dav taught himself how to watercolour
when he was making the Dragon books?
He went to the supermarket, bought a children's watercolour
set, and used it to paint the entire book series.